A NEW SCHOOL
FOR CHARLIE

COURTNEY DICMAS

For Grace and Stella – a sister is a friend for life.

First published in 2019 by Child's Play (International) Ltd
Ashworth Road, Bridgemead, Swindon SN5 7YD, UK

Published in USA by Child's Play Inc
250 Minot Avenue, Auburn, Maine 04210

Distributed in Australia by Child's Play Australia Pty Ltd
Unit 10/20 Narabang Way, Belrose, Sydney, NSW 2085

Text and illustrations copyright ©2019 Courtney Dicmas
The moral right of the author/illustrator has been asserted

ISBN 978-1-78628-341-2
CLP170419CPL06193412

Printed in Shenzhen, China

1 3 5 7 9 10 8 6 4 2

A catalogue record of this book
is available from the British Library

www.childs-play.com

BOY!

OH BOY!

BOY!

Today is Charlie's
first day at a new school.

Charlie loves everything about school.

Getting ready in the morning...

the smell
of fresh pencils,

and new
library books!

Most of all, Charlie loves
making new friends.

CATFORD PRIMARY

But at the new school, things looked very different.

The bathrooms were confusing...

and Charlie didn't know which classroom to go in.

BIRDS
of the WORLD

MR. CALICO'S
ROOM

When Charlie finally found the right room, things were very different!

Charlie tried to make friends in music class,

and again in PE.

At playtime, things went from bad to worse.

Charlie had never felt so alone.

That night at home, Charlie sat down to have a think.

"I haven't made a single friend at school."

"How can I make friends when I feel so different?"

The next day,
Charlie went to
the school library
to get some answers.

ALL About CATS

CAT FACTS

CAT CAPERS

DOG to CAT
DICTIONARY

At lunch, Charlie looked
for an empty seat.

"HEEEEEY, Charlie!"
shouted Fiona.
"You can sit right here!"

"Hi Charlie! It's nice to see you again," said Fiona.
"It's really great to see you, too!" said Charlie.

After lunch, Charlie went to art class with Fiona.
It turned out they both loved to paint.

In foreign language class, Charlie helped the teacher.

At swimming lessons, he was
the only one not afraid of water.

By the end of the day, everyone had top marks in nap class.

As time went on,
Charlie did rather
well in music class.

Things got better in PE...

and playtime was the BEST!

These days, Charlie has lots of friends at school,
but he still remembers how it felt to be lonely.

CATFORD PRIMARY

So, every day Charlie tries to make new friends!